Eddie's Dream

Mayra E. Perrony

Copyright © 2025 by Mayra E Perrony

All Rights Reserved. No part of this book, including text, illustrations, and design, may be reproduced, stored in a retrieval system, or transmitted in any form or by any means—electronic, mechanical, photocopying, recording, or otherwise—without the prior written permission of the author, except for brief quotations used in reviews or academic citations.

This work is a product of the author's creativity and is protected under international copyright laws. Unauthorized use, reproduction, or distribution of any part of this book is strictly prohibited and may result in legal action.

EBOOK: 978-1-966131-40-3

PAPERBACK: 978-1-966131-41-0

Published by Author Publications: 2025

https://www.authorpublications.com

+1 (771) 203-5560

Dedication

To my husband, who has been my inspiration and greatest supporter. To my children and grandchildren, the light of my life – this book is for you – keep dreaming and remember there's nothing you can't achieve. To the friend who believed in me even when I didn't – thanks for the push!

Acknowledgment

I would like to thank Sean Donovan and his entire team at Author's Publications for their insightful feedback and for making my vision of this book a reality.

About the Author

Mayra is a devoted grandmother of three with a heart full of love and a family full of car enthusiasts. A lifelong reader and passionate traveler, she finds joy in exploring new places and stories. In her spare time, Mayra has been making her dream come true—bringing her first children's book to life. She hopes her book will inspire young readers and dreamers of all ages to believe in themselves and chase their aspirations.

Eddie was a boy with a heart full of dreams and a spirit fueled by speed. Growing up in a small town, he found his first taste of racing on two wheels. His trusty bike was his ticket to adventure. He would ride it for hours, feeling the wind whip through his hair, the world around him a blur of green and brown.

But it wasn't just riding that excited him; he loved tinkering with his bike, too. Whenever the chain would break, or the brakes needed adjusting, Eddie would immediately roll up his sleeves, dive into the mechanics, and quickly fix it. His friends would also gather around, impressed by his skills, and soon, he became the go-to guy in town for bike repairs.

As Eddie grew older, the love for rusty two-wheelers changed to the thrill of the open road. It became even more appealing. He couldn't wait to get his driver's license, counting down the days until he turned eighteen. The moment arrived, and with determination in his eyes, he aced the driving test. He flashed his widest grin and jumped for joy when he passed on his first try.

driving license

His father, recognizing Eddie's passion, surprised him with a beat-up old car—a classic that had seen better days but was bursting with possibilities.

Eddie stood outside his garage, eyes wide with excitement as he gazed at the red car. It wasn't brand new, but to Eddie, it was special. He could see its potential. He immediately ran to inspect the car, mumbling thank yous to his Dad. He started working on it right away, fixing everything he could to make it run faster. Still, he wasn't sure if he had fixed everything, and he wanted to be sure nothing was missing.

"Dad! Come check this out!" Eddie shouted as he wiped his greasy hands on a filthy rag, his voice full of excitement.

From inside the house, his dad called back, "What's up, Eddie? Did you get the car to work?"

Eddie grinned and nodded. "Yep! It's running great now! But I need your help with one more thing. Can you come look?"

His dad walked outside, wiping his hands on his pants. He looked at Eddie and the car. "Alright, what's going on?" he asked.

Eddie bounced on his feet, practically bursting with energy. "It's running fine, but I want it to go super–fast! Like a rocket!" He pointed at the car. "I was thinking, maybe you can help me make it zoom even quicker!"

His dad smiled and nodded. "I see you're excited! Well, we can make it faster, but remember, it's not just about making the car go fast. You also have to make sure it doesn't crash when you're racing."

Eddie's eyes widened, putting him in thought for a moment. "Oh yeah, I forgot about that!" he said, scratching his head. "So, what should I do first?"

"Well," his dad said, "the engine is good, but we need to make sure the car can breathe better so it can go faster and make the wheels and shocks stronger so it doesn't bounce around too much when you turn."

Eddie nodded eagerly. "Got it! Thanks, Dad!"

Feeling even more excited, Eddie got to work. He spent countless weekends in the garage, carefully making the changes his dad suggested. He transformed that old car into something special. Finally, after weeks of hard work, the car was done. Eddie turned on the engine, and boy, did it roar! He knew that with his dad's guidance, his car would be the fastest one out there.

Eddie's talent for fixing cars continued to grow. He became a certified auto technician, earning respect for his skills and dedication. But while fixing cars was rewarding, Eddie's heart still raced for one dream: car racing. He had heard about the excitement of the Englishtown Car Races and felt the thrill of it run through his veins. With a little encouragement from his friends and family, he decided to take the plunge and participate.

The day of his first race arrived, and Eddie was both excited and nervous. His father noticed this and said right before Eddie got in the car, "Speed is great, but control is better. Stay calm and focused, have fun, and be careful out there—you got this!"

Eddie nodded, his voice filled with determination. "I 'll be careful. I promise. I 'm going to win this race!"

His dad chuckled and patted him on the back. "I 'll see you at the winning line!"

Eddie stood at the starting line, adrenaline buzzing through his veins. The roar of the engines filled the air, vibrating through his chest, while the scent of burning rubber mixed with the sharp tang of gasoline. Eddie gripped the steering wheel firmly, remembering all those moments spent dreaming of this very day.

The engines roared to life, blasting through the air, and the ground seemed to shake beneath Eddie's feet. Smoke curled from the tires as they screeched across the track in preparation, and the smell of smoking tires mixed with the fresh, crisp air.

The noise from the other cars and the people in the stands made Eddie's pulse race faster. His hands clenched the steering wheel a little tighter, and the heat from the engines seemed to wrap around him.

The world blurred into a dizzying swirl of speed and motion, the bright flash of colors from the cars streaking past him. The crowd's cheers rumbled like thunder in his ears. Every fiber of his being was alive with excitement, and the thrill of the race ignited a fire deep inside him.

As Eddie raced, his heart pounded in rhythm with the engine. The noise of the other cars and the buzz of the crowd intensified his focus. With each shift of the gears, he surged forward, gaining ground on the other drivers. His years of practice and dedication were paying off, and he could feel it with every moment. Finally, as the finish line neared, seeing the black and white checkered flag, Eddie put everything into that last burst of speed.

VICTORY LANE

1st Place: Eddie

Congratulations!!

When Eddie crossed the finish line, it was almost too much to believe—he had won! And on his birthday, no less!

The trophy gleamed in his hands, a shining symbol of his hard work and determination.

His friends and family cheered, "Congratulations! You did it!"

Their voices rang out in excitement, and Eddie's chest swelled with pride. He had transformed from a boy who fixed bikes to a champion racer, fulfilling a dream he'd held since childhood.

CONGRATS

That trophy wasn't just a victory; it was proof that with passion and perseverance, dreams could indeed become reality. Eddie knew that this was only the beginning of his racing journey. He couldn't wait to see where the road would take him next.

www.ingramcontent.com/pod-product-compliance
Lightning Source LLC
Chambersburg PA
CBHW071445300726
48976CB00004B/1444